CW00926001

Breathless Desire

Breathless Desire

A Tale of Passion and Obsession

IVY BLAIR

RWG Publishing

CONTENTS

1 | Chapter 1: A Chance Encounter   1

2 | Chapter 2: The Fire Within   3

3 | Chapter 3: A Slow Burn   6

4 | Chapter 4: The First Kiss   9

5 | Chapter 5: A Forbidden Romance   11

6 | Chapter 6: The Lure of Danger   14

7 | Chapter 7: Secrets and Lies   16

8 | Chapter 8: A Dangerous Obsession   18

9 | Chapter 9: The Price of Passion   21

10 | Chapter 10: A Risky Proposition   24

11 | Chapter 11: Playing with Fire   26

12 | Chapter 12: The Point of No Return   28

CONTENTS

13 | Chapter 13: The Thrill of the Chase   30

14 | Chapter 14: The Heat of the Moment   32

15 | Chapter 15: A Reckless Decision   34

16 | Chapter 16: The Temptation of Power   36

17 | Chapter 17: A Dark Confession   38

18 | Chapter 18: The Weight of Guilt   40

19 | Chapter 19: The Abyss of Despair   42

20 | Chapter 20: The Battle Within   44

21 | Chapter 21: The Consequences of Desire   46

22 | Chapter 22: The Long Road to Redemption   48

23 | Chapter 23: The Hope for Forgiveness   50

24 | Chapter 24: The Road to Healing   52

25 | Chapter 25: A New Beginning   54

26 | Chapter 26: Forever in Breathless Desire   56

Copyright © 2024 by IVY BLAIR

All rights reserved. No part of this book may be reproduced in any manner whatsoever without written permission except in the case of brief quotations embodied in critical articles and reviews.

First Printing, 2024

Chapter 1: A Chance Encounter

Emily's day began in the usual manner. She woke up in the morning, prepared herself for work, and hurriedly left her house to catch the bus. Despite the demanding hours spent at the office, she found great satisfaction in her job and cherished the camaraderie with her colleagues. Following a hectic day, Emily was prepared to return home and unwind.

While waiting at the bus stop, she observed a man positioned a short distance from her. He possessed a height that commanded attention, complemented by a refined sense of style. His dark locks and striking blue eyes added to his overall appeal. Emily was inexplicably intrigued by his presence, prompting her curiosity about his identity and purpose.

Unexpectedly, the man swiftly shifted his gaze and made eye contact with her. Emily's face turned red as she averted her gaze, experiencing a sense of embarrassment. She aimed to strike a balance between politeness and avoiding excessive enthusiasm. She returned her attention to the bus stop sign, patiently awaiting the arrival of her bus.

As they sat in silence, Emily occasionally glanced at the man. His gaze was focused on a distant object, indicating deep contemplation. Emily pondered the thoughts occupying his mind, and an inexplicable inclination to engage in conversation with him arose within her.

At that moment, the bus pulled up and Emily boarded, slightly let down that she missed the opportunity to converse with the gentleman. She settled into her chair and retrieved her book, fully engrossed in the narrative. However, she couldn't help but steal glances every now and then, in the hopes of catching another glimpse of the man she saw at the bus stop.

While traveling on the bus, Emily had a persistent intuition that she was destined to encounter the man. For reasons unknown, his presence had captivated her.

Ultimately, as they neared Emily's destination, she made a daring choice. She collected her belongings and rose from her seat, making her way towards the front of the bus. As she walked by the man, she inhaled deeply and addressed him.

"Pardon me," she stated, "I couldn't help but observe your presence at the bus stop." Would you be interested in meeting for a coffee at some point?

The man appeared taken aback yet also captivated. He smiled and said, "I'd like that very much."

Emily's heart fluttered as she exchanged numbers with the man. She was astonished by her boldness in asking a stranger out, yet she couldn't ignore the thrill coursing through her.

As she walked off the bus, Emily turned back and caught the man's eye. She smiled, experiencing a sense of excitement. She was uncertain about the future implications of this unexpected meeting, but she felt a sense of anticipation to discover what lay ahead.

Chapter 2: The Fire Within

Emily's pulse quickened as she contemplated the gentleman she had encountered at the bus stop. They had exchanged contact information and scheduled a coffee meeting for later in the week. Emily was taken aback by her audacity, yet she couldn't ignore the strong pull she felt towards the man.

Over time, Emily's thoughts became increasingly consumed by the man. She pondered his character, occupation, and relationship preferences. She attempted to maintain composure, yet internally, she was consumed by a fervent longing.

At last, the long-awaited day of their coffee date arrived, and Emily experienced a blend of anticipation and jitters as she headed towards the café. As she noticed the man seated by the window, her heart raced with anticipation as she made her way towards him.

"Hello," she replied, slightly breathless. "Thank you for taking the time to meet with me."

The individual displayed a pleasant facial expression and rose from his seat. "I am pleased to assist," he stated, indicating for her to sit down. "May I offer you a beverage?"

They engaged in conversation over coffee, exchanging personal anecdotes and getting acquainted. Emily was captivated by the man's self-assured demeanor and quick intelligence. He possessed a remarkable intellect, a delightful sense of humor, and an irresistible charm, which ignited a palpable attraction within her.

After finishing their drinks, the man turned to Emily and expressed, "I don't mean to be presumptuous, but I sense a certain connection between us." Are you interested in going on a formal date in the future?

Emily's pulse quickened as she replied, "Certainly, that would be most delightful."

Emily and the man started a romantic relationship. They engaged in various social activities, such as dining out, watching films, and discovering the city. Emily was astonished by the striking similarities she shared with him, and she perceived a profound level of understanding from him that surpassed any previous experiences.

However, as their relationship grew stronger, Emily started to experience a sense of passion. She desired a deeper connection with the man, beyond mere social outings and superficial discussions. She desired the sensation of his touch, the intimacy of closeness, and the connection of a profound shared experience.

While enjoying a leisurely afternoon in the park, Emily mustered the bravery to articulate her emotions.

"Listen," she stated, inhaling deeply. "I want to provide you with an honest perspective, without causing any alarm." I sense a connection between us, a growing bond that has been developing since our initial encounter. I am uncertain about the future direction of our relationship, but I must admit that I desire a deeper connection with you beyond mere friendship.

The man glanced at Emily, his demeanor displaying a sense of gravity. "I share the same sentiment," he stated. "I have attempted to restrain myself, however, it is undeniable that I am experiencing a profound attraction towards you."

Emily experienced a sudden surge of emotion when the man drew closer and initiated a kiss. The kiss was tender and delicate, yet it ignited an intense wave of longing within her. She experienced an intensifying passion, recognizing a person capable of fulfilling her most profound longings.

Chapter 3: A Slow Burn

Emily and the man had deepened their relationship, and she was overwhelmed by a newfound intensity of emotion. They dedicated their time to thoroughly exploring one another, uncovering new aspects of themselves and their relationship.

However, as the initial excitement of their new relationship waned, Emily came to the realization that there was a more profound connection between them. They had a deep connection that transcended mere physical attraction, a bond that appeared to strengthen with each passing day.

Emily and the man frequently engaged in intimate conversations on the couch, discussing their aspirations, anxieties, and profound longings. They exchanged anecdotes about their upbringing, their familial backgrounds, and their previous romantic involvements. They developed a deep emotional connection that was previously unexplored, leading Emily to believe she had discovered her perfect match.

As their relationship progressed, Emily started to observe a distinct change in the man. It appeared that he was withholding, concealing a portion of himself from her. She lacked knowledge of its nature, yet she possessed an awareness that he was withholding information from her.

Emily attempted to engage in conversation with the man regarding the matter, yet he consistently evaded her inquiries. He would divert the conversation, employ humor, or express his desire to preserve their impeccable relationship. However, Emily sensed a discrepancy, which gradually started to trouble her.

During a shared moment in bed, Emily made the decision to address the man.

"Listen," she stated, gazing into his eyes. "I am aware that there is information you have chosen not to disclose." I sense its presence. Please feel free to share with me. I am seeking accurate information.

Emily caught the man's gaze, noting the unmistakable sorrow in his eyes. "I regret my inability to provide you with the information," he stated. "However, there are certain aspects of my past that I regret." Experiences that have left an indelible mark on my memory, both the things I have done and the things I have witnessed. I don't wish to impose them upon you.

Emily experienced a surge of compassion. It was evident that the man had experienced a challenging ordeal, one that had left a lasting impact on him. She was uncertain of its nature, yet driven by a desire to aid in his recovery.

"Please listen," she stated, gently grasping his hand. "I understand that you have experienced a challenging situation." I don't expect you to provide me with all the information at this moment. I want to assure you that I am available to support you. I am committed to providing support and assistance to facilitate your healing process, tailoring my approach to meet your specific needs.

The man gazed at Emily, his eyes brimming with sentiment. "You are an exceptional individual," he stated. "I am uncertain of the actions I took that led to your presence in my life."

From that point forward, Emily and the man's relationship underwent a significant transformation. They collaborated to assist him in recovering from his previous traumas, and Emily discovered that her affection for him grew stronger with each passing day. The relationship gradually developed, becoming more solid over time, and was founded on trust, love, and acceptance.

4

Chapter 4: The First Kiss

Emily's bond with the man had strengthened over time, and her feelings for him had intensified. They frequently spent their leisure time together, engaging in urban exploration, sampling novel culinary establishments, and exchanging aspirations and ambitions.

During their evening stroll, the man halted Emily on the street. He gazed at her, his eyes brimming with sentiment, and gently grasped her hand.

"Emily," he stated, "there is a matter I must discuss with you."

Emily's heart fluttered as she gazed into the man's eyes. Recognizing the gravity of the situation, she anxiously anticipated his next words.

"I have strong feelings for you," he murmured softly.

Emily experienced a surge of sentiment engulfing her. She had long been aware of her love for the man, but his verbal affirmation made it feel even more tangible.

"I reciprocate your feelings," she expressed, gently grasping the man's hand.

The man embraced her tightly and planted a passionate kiss on her lips. The kiss was characterized by its gentle and tender nature, conveying a deep sense of affection. Emily sensed the gentle touch of the man's lips meeting hers, signaling the start of their shared path.

As they said goodbye, Emily glanced up at the man and offered a warm smile. She was aware that their relationship was in its early stages, yet she recognized the significance of this moment, one that would remain etched in her memory. The initial kiss marked the beginning of a love that would endure for a lifetime.

5

Chapter 5: A Forbidden Romance

Emily and the man had developed a strong and intense romantic connection. They frequently engaged in shared activities, such as venturing to unfamiliar locations, experimenting with novel experiences, and relishing each other's companionship.

However, a complication arose: the man was already married.

Emily was aware of the man's marital status from the start, yet she never anticipated developing romantic feelings for him. Despite her initial efforts to maintain a strictly platonic relationship, the man's irresistible charm and charisma eventually captivated her.

Emily persisted in maintaining a clandestine relationship with the man, despite her reservations. They would discreetly rendezvous, clandestinely stealing moments whenever possible.

Emily was aware of the moral implications of their actions, yet she found herself unable to control her emotions. She had strong feelings for the man and couldn't envision her life without him.

Over time, Emily gradually became aware of the flaws in the man's seemingly perfect marriage. He would share his personal struggles with her, discussing his difficult family situation, his troubled relationship, and his longing to be with her.

Emily was aware of the necessity to terminate her relationship with the man, recognizing the need to distance herself from the illicit affair. However, she was unable to muster the courage to complete the task. She had strong feelings for him and believed that their relationship was destined.

During a private moment, the man expressed his desire to end his marriage and be with Emily.

"Emily," he expressed, "I am unable to continue my existence in your absence. I desire to be by your side, to construct a future together. I am willing to take any necessary steps to be with you, even if it means ending my current relationship.

Emily experienced a range of conflicting emotions. She recognized the ethical implications of the man's proposition, emphasizing the importance of prioritizing the restoration of his marriage before embarking on a new relationship. However, she couldn't ignore the strong affection she had for him and her longing for a lifelong companionship.

Ultimately, Emily made the decision to take a risk on the man. She understood the inherent risks and the forbidden nature of their relationship, yet she remained steadfast in the authenticity of their love.

They decided to leave their current lives and begin anew in a different city, where they could establish a life together. Emily was aware of the challenges and anticipated encountering numerous obstacles throughout their journey. However, she recognized her deep affection for the man and understood the significance of their relationship, which compelled her to persevere.

Ultimately, the relationship between Emily and the man served as a cautionary tale about the perils of an illicit love affair. The relationship was founded on falsehoods and deception, causing harm to numerous individuals along the way. Emily was aware of the lessons she had gained from her past errors and was determined not to repeat them. Despite the forbidden nature of their love, she was certain of its authenticity and the profound impact it had on her life.

6

Chapter 6: The Lure of Danger

The relationship between Emily and the man had deteriorated. After relocating to a different city, their expectations were not being met.

The individual resorted to substance abuse as a means of dealing with the overwhelming pressure brought upon by their recent union. Emily attempted to provide assistance and support to him during his difficulties, yet it appeared that he was experiencing a loss of stability.

Upon returning home late that evening, the man displayed bloodshot eyes and emitted the scent of alcohol from his breath. Emily sensed a discrepancy and made an effort to engage in a conversation with him, hoping to encourage him to share his thoughts and feelings. However, the individual displayed a sense of detachment, lack of engagement, and seemed consumed by their personal struggle with addiction and hopelessness.

Over time, Emily found herself increasingly attracted to the man's risky demeanor. She was aware of the moral and personal hazards associated with his actions. However, there was an intriguing allure to the man's risky lifestyle that captivated her.

Emily became entangled in the man's perilous way of life, engaging in unprecedented acts of daring. They would spend the entire night engaging in social activities, consuming alcohol, engaging in altercations, and using substances. Emily was aware of the moral implications of their actions, yet she found herself irresistibly drawn to the exhilarating sense of risk it provided.

Over time, Emily came to the realization that she couldn't resolve the man's addiction. She understood the necessity of parting ways, relinquishing the perilous existence they had shared.

Arriving at a conclusion proved to be a challenging task, causing emotional turmoil. She had deep affection for the man, yet she understood that she was unable to rescue him from his own struggles. Ultimately, Emily made the decision to depart, leaving the man behind and embarking on a new independent journey.

Despite the difficulties, Emily was aware of the necessity of her actions. She was attracted to the man's risky nature and the excitement of living life on the edge. However, she was aware that this lifestyle was not viable in the long run, as it would inevitably result in emotional distress and suffering.

Ultimately, Emily discovered the irresistible allure of danger. It has the power to captivate and invigorate, yet it can also have detrimental effects, guiding one towards a journey of self-destruction and desolation. Emily discovered the value of removing oneself from harmful situations and embarking on a fresh journey of self-reliance.

7

Chapter 7: Secrets and Lies

Emily had transitioned away from her previous relationship and embarked on a new independent journey. She had recently started a new job, made new acquaintances, and was reveling in a newfound sense of liberation that was entirely unfamiliar to her.

However, over time, Emily came to acknowledge a void in her life. She longed for the intense emotions and exhilaration that had once consumed her in the relationship, the sense of living on the edge.

Emily encountered a new individual who appeared to possess a mutual appreciation for excitement and risk. They entered into a romantic relationship, and Emily discovered herself developing strong feelings for him at a rapid pace. However, as their relationship grew stronger, Emily gradually became aware of the man's true nature.

He would frequently go missing for extended periods, leaving Emily with unanswered questions about his whereabouts and activities. He consistently deceived her regarding his personal history, occupation, and social circle, resulting in her profound sense of unfamiliarity with his true self.

Emily was inexplicably attracted to the man's risky demeanor, despite her reservations. He would lead her on exciting escapades,

| 16 |

acquainting her with unfamiliar individuals and novel encounters. Emily embraced the exhilarating sense of living on the edge once more, finding immense joy in the experience.

However, as their relationship progressed, Emily gradually became aware of the man's undisclosed secrets. She was unaware of its nature, yet she sensed a concealed darkness within him, something he was withholding from her.

During an evening at a club, Emily observed the man engaging in conversation with another woman. She experienced a surge of envy and confronted him.

"Who is she?" she inquired, her voice trembling with frustration.

The man gazed at Emily, his eyes burdened with remorse. "She is merely an acquaintance," he murmured softly.

Emily was skeptical of his statement. She was aware of his undisclosed secret, something he kept concealed from her.

Over time, Emily gradually discovered the hidden truths of the man. She discovered his previous involvement in criminal activities, including drug trafficking and theft, which resulted in a lengthy prison sentence. She came to the realization that he had deceived her from the start, revealing a stark contrast to the person she had initially perceived him to be.

Ultimately, Emily had to disengage from the individual. She found it unacceptable to be in a relationship with someone who lived a dishonest and deceptive life, concealing their true identity from her. Emily came to the realization that the excitement of risk was not worth the emotional and physical suffering it entailed.

She discovered the detrimental impact of secrecy and deception on relationships, as they undermine trust and inflict lasting harm. She recognized the importance of being truthful and authentic, both to herself and to those around her. It was clear to her that this was the most beneficial course of action.

8

Chapter 8: A Dangerous Obsession

Emily had transitioned from her previous romantic connections and was relishing in her recently acquired autonomy. She possessed a fulfilling occupation, a remarkable circle of acquaintances, and a profound sense of direction that was previously unfamiliar to her.

However, Emily's life took a significant turn when she encountered a man who would have a profound impact on her. He possessed an irresistible allure, with his charm, charisma, and a hint of danger. Emily couldn't resist her attraction to him, even though she knew it wasn't wise.

After entering into a romantic relationship, Emily experienced a renewed sense of excitement and thrill. The man would lead her on exciting escapades, acquaint her with unfamiliar individuals, and expose her to a realm of existence she had yet to encounter.

However, as their relationship progressed, Emily gradually became aware of the man's alarming tendencies and his intense fixation. He frequently contacted her, appearing at her place of employment, and inquiring about her whereabouts and companions.

Emily attempted to disregard the indications of trouble, convincing herself that the man's actions were merely a manifestation of his intense affection for her. However, as time passed, the man's fixation intensified, causing Emily to feel trapped in a never-ending nightmare.

She attempted to terminate the relationship, but he adamantly resisted releasing her. He would frequently appear at her residence, send her intimidating messages, and instill a constant sense of insecurity.

Emily recognized the need to take measures to ensure her own safety. She sought support from her friends, who assisted her in obtaining a legal order of protection against the individual. She altered her phone number, relocated to a new apartment, and endeavored to progress in her life.

However, the man's fixation proved to be quite persistent. He persistently attempted to reach out to Emily, appearing at her workplace, and instilling a constant sense of insecurity.

Ultimately, Emily came to the realization that she had to take significant measures. She enlisted the services of a private investigator to delve into the individual's history, leading to the discovery of profoundly unsettling revelations.

Emily became aware of the man's violent and stalking tendencies, and she came to the realization that she had narrowly evaded a perilous situation. She understood the necessity of distancing herself from him, severing all ties with him.

Emily was filled with fear and vulnerability as she grappled with the challenging choice before her. However, she understood that it was necessary to safeguard herself and prevent any future encounters with a perilous fixation.

Emily discovered that the allure of perilous situations can often indicate a deeper, more troubling reality. She understood the significance of heeding her instincts, relying on her intuition, and prioritizing her personal safety and well-being.

Chapter 9: The Price of Passion

Emily has experienced significant challenges in her previous romantic partnerships. She experienced the tumultuous journey of love, faced deception, and managed to break free from a perilous fixation.

However, despite all circumstances, she maintained her unwavering faith in the transformative potential of love. She sought a compatible partner who shared her enthusiasm and embraced her true self.

Emily encountered an individual who appeared to meet her requirements. He possessed qualities of kindness, compassion, and a profound passion for exploration and thrill. Emily believed she had discovered a kindred spirit, someone who comprehended her deeply and could partake in her aspirations and interests.

As their bond grew stronger, Emily came to the realization that the man she had been seeking had finally appeared in her life. He embodied all the qualities she desired in a partner, and her affection for him was profound.

However, as their relationship progressed, Emily started to acknowledge the consequences that came with their intense emotions. The individual was consistently active, continuously pursuing novel experiences and exhilarating adventures. He had a tendency to spend money without much thought, often taking risks and embracing a carefree lifestyle.

Emily endeavored to match the man's enthusiasm and zest for life, striving to keep pace with him. However, as time progressed, she started to experience a sense of losing her own identity in the midst of it all. She was making financial decisions without sufficient funds, engaging in activities outside her comfort zone, and making compromises on her principles and convictions.

At a certain point, Emily became unable to match the pace of the man. She was aware of her feelings for him, yet she recognized the importance of prioritizing her own well-being. She engaged in a sincere and meaningful discussion with the man.

"I must express that I have deep affection for you, however, I find it challenging to maintain pace with you any longer," she stated. I must prioritize self-care, embrace a slower pace, and direct my attention towards the aspects of life that hold significance to me.

Upon careful reflection, the man came to the realization that he had been neglecting Emily's importance in his life. He had been too engrossed in his personal passion and thirst for adventure to pause and contemplate the impact it had on those around him.

Ultimately, the man and Emily collaborated to achieve a harmonious equilibrium. They continued to pursue adventure and excitement, but in a responsible and sustainable manner. They dedicated themselves to valuing one another and their connection, prioritizing what truly held significance.

Emily discovered the potential consequences of pursuing one's passions, emphasizing the significance of maintaining a harmonious equilibrium between personal fulfillment and the well-being of loved ones. She was confident in her ability to face any challenge that life presented, thanks to the support of her partner.

Chapter 10: A Risky Proposition

Emily had rediscovered love and basked in its happiness. However, as time unfolded, an unmistakable void crept into her life. Always one to yearn for adventure and thrill, she sensed being mired in monotony.

Then, fate introduced Emily to a man who would revolutionize everything. Charismatic and daring, he laid out a tantalizing proposal.

This man was a professional gambler seeking a partner to conquer the casinos. Intrigued, Emily sensed it could be the excitement she craved. They embarked on this journey together, and Emily found herself engulfed in the world of gambling. Hours melted away at the tables, chasing the elusive victory against the odds.

Initially cautious, Emily recognized the risks inherent in gambling – a perilous path where everything could be lost. Yet, with time, she felt the rush of success, a feeling of invincibility.

Hours were devoted to studying odds, analyzing games, and devising strategies. Emily felt she had reached the pinnacle, finally discovering the thrill and adventure she longed for.

However, as their gambling persisted, Emily grasped the inherent danger. They were gambling away not just money but their savings and future. Emily foresaw the impending loss of everything they had worked for.

In the end, Emily faced a poignant decision. She realized the allure of the risky proposition wasn't worth the sacrifice; she couldn't continue to gamble away her future.

Walking away from both the man and the gambling world, Emily vowed to find a new avenue for adventure and excitement. Though challenging, she knew it was the right choice.

The experience taught her a crucial lesson – the risks we undertake can be more perilous than anticipated, leading us down a path of self-destruction. Emily understood the importance of striking a balance between excitement and responsibility, taking risks without jeopardizing everything one holds dear.

11

Chapter 11: Playing with Fire

Having distanced herself from the world of gambling, Emily sought new avenues to satisfy her craving for excitement and adventure. She delved into a fresh job, embraced new hobbies, and reveled in her newfound freedom.

Then, one day, she encountered a man who would redefine everything. A firefighter with an irresistible dangerous edge.

Their romance unfolded, and Emily found herself living on the edge once more. The man whisked her away on thrilling adventures, introduced her to new circles, and revealed facets of life she had never known.

In him, Emily sensed a kindred spirit who understood her, someone to share in her passion and zest for life.

As their relationship deepened, Emily grappled with the realization that the man's job was far more perilous than she had imagined. He braved burning buildings, risking his life to save others. The fear took hold that one day, he might not return.

Despite her concerns, Emily endeavored to support him in his perilous job. Visiting the fire station, bringing supplies, and assisting in any way possible became her routine.

Yet, with time, Emily confronted the harsh truth that her love for the man was putting her in jeopardy. She followed him into burning buildings, attempted to assist in firefighting, and willingly exposed herself to risk.

In the end, a difficult decision loomed for Emily. She recognized that the thrill of danger wasn't worth endangering her own life. Though she loved the man deeply, she couldn't persist in jeopardizing herself.

In a heart-to-heart conversation, Emily expressed her feelings to the man. "I love you, but I can't keep putting myself in danger like this. I need to take care of myself, to focus on the things that matter to me."

Acknowledging his role in endangering Emily, the man apologized. Together, they worked to find a new equilibrium.

They continued their adventures, but now in a manner that prioritized responsibility and safety. Emily understood that her love for the man should not compromise her own well-being.

Through this experience, Emily learned the significance of taking risks responsibly and sustainably. With the man by her side, she felt ready to face whatever challenges life presented.

Chapter 12: The Point of No Return

Emily had traversed a myriad of experiences, from the highs of love to narrowly escaping danger. Throughout it all, she endeavored to remain true to herself, living a life of authenticity and purpose.

Then, one day, Emily encountered a man who would challenge the very essence of her being. Mysterious, intriguing, with a dark edge that proved irresistible.

As they delved into a romantic relationship, Emily found herself immersed in the man's passion and thirst for adventure. It felt like she had finally discovered a kindred spirit, someone who comprehended her dreams and shared her passions.

Yet, as their connection deepened, Emily began to realize that the man was steering her towards a perilous path. He exposed her to risky situations, urged her to undertake uncomfortable tasks, and made her feel as if she were losing control of her own life.

Despite her reservations, Emily continued down this dangerous path, living on the edge and embracing the excitement and passion she had always craved.

Over time, however, Emily grasped the gravity of her situation, realizing she had crossed a line, gone too far down a dangerous path from which she couldn't turn back, unable to escape the man's grasp.

Recognizing the need to protect herself, Emily confided in friends who urged her to leave the man and forge a new life. Yet, Emily found herself unable to sever ties. Deeply in love, she believed she couldn't live without him, despite the dangerous circumstances.

Inevitably, Emily faced the consequences of her choices. Arrested for participating in the man's illegal activities, she confronted a lengthy prison sentence.

It was a harsh lesson, leaving Emily with regret and remorse. She acknowledged her mistake, understanding that her yearning for adventure and excitement had clouded her judgment.

Even in her darkest hour, Emily clung to hope. She knew she could turn her life around, make better choices, and start anew.

Her journey taught her that the path of danger might lead to a point of no return. To avoid it, Emily learned to listen to her instincts, trust her gut, and never compromise on her values and beliefs.

Top of Form

Chapter 13: The Thrill of the Chase

Emily had encountered various experiences in her life, from falling in love to narrowly escaping danger. Throughout it all, she remained someone who harbored a deep-seated craving for excitement and adventure.

One day, she met a man who would challenge her perceptions of herself. A dedicated hunter with a passion for the outdoors that proved irresistible to Emily.

As they entered into a romantic relationship, Emily found herself immersed in the man's fervor for the chase. He took her on hunting trips, taught her to track animals, and imparted survival skills for the wilderness.

In him, Emily felt a connection, someone who shared her love for adventure and excitement.

However, as their relationship deepened, Emily came to understand that the man's passion carried more danger than she had initially realized. He took risks, put himself in harm's way, and made her feel constantly on edge.

Despite her fears, Emily continued down this perilous path, relishing the thrill and passion she had long sought.

Yet, with time, Emily recognized that she had crossed a line, jeopardizing not only her life but also the lives of the animals they pursued.

Facing a difficult decision, Emily knew she loved the man, but she couldn't persist in endangering herself.

In a heart-to-heart conversation, she expressed her feelings to the man. "Listen," she said, "I love you, but I can't keep putting myself in danger like this. I need to take care of myself, to focus on the things that matter to me."

The man listened, acknowledging his role in putting Emily at risk. He apologized, and together, they sought a new balance.

While they still embarked on hunting trips, they did so responsibly and sustainably. Emily understood her love for the man, but she refused to let it compromise her safety.

In the end, Emily learned that the thrill of the chase could be dangerous. She realized the importance of taking risks responsibly and sustainably. With the man by her side, she felt ready to face whatever challenges life presented.

14 ▌

Chapter 14: The Heat of the Moment

Emily had navigated a spectrum of experiences, from falling in love to narrowly escaping danger. Throughout it all, she remained someone with an enduring craving for excitement and adventure.

One day, she encountered a man who would challenge the core of her being. A firefighter with an unwavering passion for extinguishing fires, a calling that captivated Emily.

As their romance unfolded, Emily found herself immersed in the man's fervor for helping others. She felt a profound connection, finally discovering someone who comprehended her love for adventure and excitement.

However, as their relationship deepened, Emily grappled with the realization that the man's job was more perilous than she had initially imagined. He courageously entered burning buildings, risking his life to save others. The fear lingered that one day, he might not return.

Despite her apprehensions, Emily continued down the path of danger, relishing the thrill and passion she had long sought.

Yet, with time, Emily acknowledged that she had crossed a line, jeopardizing not only her life but also the life of the man she loved.

In a decisive moment, Emily knew she had to take action to protect both herself and the man she loved. In a heartfelt conversation, she expressed her concerns.

"Listen," she said, "I love you, but I can't keep putting myself and you in danger like this. I need to take care of myself, to focus on the things that matter to me."

The man listened, realizing he had inadvertently endangered Emily. He apologized, and together, they sought a new equilibrium.

While they continued their adventures, they did so responsibly and safely. Emily understood her love for the man, but she refused to let it jeopardize their lives.

In the end, Emily learned that the heat of the moment could be perilous. She grasped the importance of taking risks responsibly and sustainably. With the man by her side, she felt ready to face whatever challenges life presented.

15

Chapter 15: A Reckless Decision

Emily had weathered numerous experiences in her life, from falling in love to narrowly escaping danger. Throughout it all, she remained someone with an insatiable craving for excitement and adventure.

One day, she encountered a man who would challenge the very core of her identity. He was impulsive, reckless, and possessed a passion for living life on the edge.

As they embarked on a romantic journey, Emily found herself caught up in the man's fervor for adventure. It seemed she had finally discovered someone who understood and shared her love for excitement and thrill.

However, as their relationship deepened, Emily came to realize that the man's impulsiveness was more perilous than she had ever imagined. He embraced risks, placed himself in harm's way, and made her feel constantly on edge.

Despite her fears, Emily continued to follow the man down this hazardous path, relishing the sense of living on the edge and experiencing the excitement and passion she had always yearned for.

Yet, with time, Emily acknowledged that her decision to follow the man was reckless. She was putting herself in danger and jeopardizing everything she had worked for.

Faced with a difficult choice, Emily knew she loved the man, but she couldn't persist in endangering herself. In a heart-to-heart conversation, she expressed her feelings.

"Listen," she said, "I love you, but I can't keep putting myself in danger like this. I need to take care of myself, to focus on the things that matter to me."

The man listened, but it seemed he didn't fully grasp the gravity of Emily's concerns. He persisted in pushing her to take risks, live on the edge, and follow him down the perilous path.

Ultimately, Emily realized she had to walk away from the man, no matter how deep her love for him. She understood that she couldn't continue putting herself in danger, needing to prioritize her well-being and future.

From this experience, Emily learned that a reckless decision could have serious consequences. She grasped the importance of taking risks responsibly and sustainably. Armed with these lessons, she felt prepared to face whatever challenges life had in store.

16

Chapter 16: The Temptation of Power

Emily had always been someone who craved excitement and adventure, and she held a deep appreciation for integrity and honesty.

One day, she encountered a man who would challenge the very essence of her identity. Powerful, influential, and driven by a passion for manipulation, he enticed Emily into his world.

As their relationship unfolded, Emily found herself immersed in the man's power and his quest for control. She believed she had finally found someone who could provide the life she had always dreamed of.

However, as their connection deepened, Emily began to realize that the man's influence was more perilous than she had initially imagined. He wielded his power to control others, manipulate situations, and left Emily feeling like she was losing control of her own life.

Despite her reservations, Emily continued down the path of power, savoring the excitement and passion she had long yearned for.

Yet, with time, Emily acknowledged that she had crossed a line, compromising her integrity, honesty, and sense of self.

In the end, Emily faced a challenging decision. She loved the man, but she couldn't continue to compromise her values and beliefs.

In a heartfelt conversation, she expressed her feelings to the man. "Listen," she said, "I love you, but I can't keep compromising my integrity like this. I need to take care of myself, to focus on the things that matter to me."

The man listened, but understanding seemed elusive. He persisted in pushing Emily to use her power, manipulate others, and follow him down the path of control.

Ultimately, Emily realized she had to walk away from the man, despite her deep love for him. She recognized the need to uphold her values and prioritize her well-being and future.

From this experience, Emily learned that the allure of power can be dangerous, underscoring the importance of staying true to oneself and one's values. Equipped with these lessons, she felt prepared to face whatever challenges life had in store.

Chapter 17: A Dark Confession

Emily had faced a myriad of experiences in her life, from falling in love to narrowly escaping danger. Throughout it all, she had consistently held honesty and integrity in high regard.

One day, Emily encountered a man who would challenge the very core of her identity. Charming, handsome, with a mysterious allure and a dark secret she couldn't resist.

As they delved into a romantic relationship, Emily found herself captivated by the man's passion and enigmatic nature. It felt like she had finally discovered someone who comprehended and shared her love for excitement and thrill.

However, as their connection deepened, Emily began to sense that the man was concealing something from her. He would disappear for extended periods, evade her questions, and erode the trust she had in him.

Despite her apprehensions, Emily continued down the perilous path with the man. She believed she was living on the edge, finally experiencing the excitement and passion she had always craved.

Yet, with time, Emily realized that the man's secret was more dangerous than she had ever imagined. He was entangled in illegal activities, and unwittingly, she was aiding him.

In the end, Emily confronted the man about his secret. In a heart-to-heart conversation, she expressed her feelings.

"Listen," she said, "I love you, but I can't keep living a lie like this. I need you to be honest with me, to tell me the truth."

The man listened and finally confessed, revealing his involvement in illegal activities and the double life he had been leading.

Emily was shocked, yet a sense of relief washed over her. She understood she couldn't continue living a lie, realizing the need to take control of her life and make better choices.

Ultimately, Emily chose to walk away from the man, recognizing that she couldn't be with someone involved in illegal activities. It was a difficult decision, but she knew it was the right one.

Emily learned that sometimes, loved ones may hide dark secrets. She realized that the key to protecting herself was to trust her instincts, be honest with herself and others, and steadfastly stay true to her values and beliefs.

Chapter 18: The Weight of Guilt

Emily had always been someone who prized honesty and integrity, but she could also be hard on herself when things didn't go according to plan.

One day, Emily met a man who would challenge everything she knew about herself. Kind, caring, and driven by a passion for helping others, he sparked a connection with Emily.

As they entered into a romantic relationship, Emily found herself immersed in the man's kindness and his desire to make a positive difference in the world. It felt like she had finally found someone who comprehended her, someone who could share her love for making a positive impact.

However, as their relationship deepened, Emily discovered that the man carried a heavy burden of guilt from mistakes in his past. He struggled to forgive himself, and despite her love for him, Emily felt weighed down by the guilt he bore.

In the end, Emily had to address the issue with the man. In a heart-to-heart conversation, she expressed her feelings.

"Listen," she said, "I love you, but I can't keep carrying the weight of your guilt. You need to forgive yourself, to let go of the past."

The man listened, recognizing that he had burdened Emily with his guilt. He apologized, and together, they worked to find a way to move forward.

They continued making a positive impact in the world, but now grounded in self-forgiveness and self-love. Emily understood her love for the man, but she also realized that she couldn't let his guilt consume her.

Ultimately, Emily learned that the weight of guilt can be burdensome. She grasped the importance of forgiveness, both for oneself and others, as a pathway to moving forward. Armed with these lessons, she felt ready to face whatever challenges life had in store.

19

Chapter 19: The Abyss of Despair

Emily had faced numerous challenges in her life, from falling in love to narrowly escaping danger. Throughout it all, she remained a resilient and hopeful individual.

One day, she encountered a man who would challenge the very essence of her being. Troubled, broken, and harboring a darkness that drew her in, he became a significant presence in her life.

As they embarked on a romantic journey, Emily found herself immersed in the man's pain and his quest for redemption. It felt like she had finally discovered someone who comprehended her, someone who could share her love for healing and growth.

However, as their relationship deepened, Emily realized that the man's darkness was more profound than she had initially imagined. Struggling with addiction, haunted by past trauma, and enveloped in a deep sense of hopelessness, he became a heavy burden on Emily's shoulders.

Despite her love for him, Emily felt overwhelmed by his despair. She sensed herself drowning in his pain, unsure of how to provide the help he needed.

In the end, Emily had to address the issue with the man. In a heart-to-heart conversation, she spoke her truth.

"Listen," she said, "I love you, but I can't keep drowning in your despair. You need to seek help, to find a way to heal."

The man listened, but the path to hope seemed elusive to him. He continued spiraling deeper into his pain, and Emily felt like she was losing him.

Ultimately, Emily faced a difficult decision. Despite her love for the man, she couldn't continue sacrificing her own well-being for his. She chose to walk away, recognizing it as the right decision. She understood that he needed to find his own way out of the abyss of despair, and she couldn't be the one to save him.

Emily learned that, at times, love alone isn't enough to rescue someone from their pain. She understood that the key to protecting herself was to trust her instincts, establish healthy boundaries, and consistently prioritize her own well-being.

20

Chapter 20: The Battle Within

Emily had always been someone who valued honesty and integrity, but she could also be hard on herself when things didn't go according to plan.

One day, Emily met a man who would challenge everything she knew about herself. Charismatic, confident, and driven by a passion for achieving success, he drew Emily into his world.

As they entered into a romantic relationship, Emily found herself swept up in the man's charisma and his fervent desire to be the best. It felt like she had finally met someone who understood her drive and ambition.

However, as their relationship deepened, Emily became aware of the man's own internal struggles. He harbored a dark side, consumed by the need to win at any cost.

Despite her love for him, Emily felt conflicted about the man's darker tendencies. She found herself in a constant internal battle, torn between her drive for success and the man's all-encompassing desire to win.

In the end, Emily had to address the issue with the man. In a heart-to-heart conversation, she expressed her feelings.

"Listen," she said, "I love you, but I can't keep fighting this internal battle. We need to find a way to balance our drive for success with our values and beliefs."

The man listened, but he seemed unsure about how to move forward. He continued pushing Emily to be more competitive, more aggressive, and to follow him down the path of winning at all costs.

Ultimately, Emily realized that she had to walk away from the man, no matter how much she loved him. She understood that she couldn't compromise her own values and beliefs, recognizing the need to find a way to succeed without sacrificing who she was.

Emily learned that the internal battle can be the most challenging one of all, emphasizing the importance of staying true to one's values and beliefs, even when faced with difficulties. Armed with these lessons, she felt ready to face anything that life had to offer.

Chapter 21: The Consequences of Desire

Emily had navigated through various experiences in her life, from falling in love to narrowly escaping danger. Throughout it all, she remained someone who yearned for excitement and passion.

One day, Emily encountered a man who would challenge the very essence of her being. Magnetic, alluring, and with an unwavering passion for living life to the fullest, he drew Emily into his world.

As they embarked on a romantic journey, Emily found herself immersed in the man's desire and magnetic allure. It felt like she had finally met someone who comprehended her, someone who could share her love for excitement and passion.

However, as their relationship deepened, Emily began to recognize the perilous nature of the man's desire. He was reckless, impulsive, and would take risks that not only jeopardized their relationship but also put her life in danger.

Despite her fears, Emily continued to follow the man down the path of desire. She felt like she was living on the edge, finally experiencing the kind of excitement and passion she had always craved.

However, as time passed, Emily began to realize the consequences of their unrestrained desire. She was jeopardizing her safety, well-being, and future.

In the end, Emily faced a difficult decision. Despite her love for the man, she knew she couldn't continue risking everything for their desire.

In a heart-to-heart conversation, she expressed her feelings to the man. "Listen," she said, "I love you, but I can't keep risking everything for our desire. We need to find a way to balance our passion with our safety and well-being."

The man listened, but the gravity of their situation seemed elusive to him. He continued to push Emily to take risks, to live on the edge, and to follow him down the path of desire.

Ultimately, Emily realized she had to walk away from the man, no matter how much she loved him. She understood that she couldn't keep risking everything for their desire and needed to find a way to experience passion and excitement in a safe and sustainable manner.

Emily learned that the consequences of unchecked desire can be severe, emphasizing the importance of balancing passion with safety and well-being. Equipped with these lessons, she felt ready to face whatever challenges life had to offer.

Chapter 22: The Long Road to Redemption

Emily had always been someone who valued honesty and integrity, but she also believed in second chances and redemption.

One day, Emily met a man who would challenge everything she knew about herself. Troubled, broken, and having made mistakes in the past, he became a significant part of her life.

As they started dating, Emily found herself immersed in the man's pain and his desire for redemption. It felt like she had finally encountered someone who not only understood her but could also share her love for healing and growth.

However, as their relationship deepened, Emily began to realize that the man's journey to redemption was going to be long and arduous. He grappled with addiction, past trauma, and a profound sense of shame.

Despite her deep love for the man, Emily couldn't help but feel overwhelmed by the enormity of his journey. She sensed that the road ahead would be challenging, and she questioned whether she had the strength to stand by his side.

In the end, Emily had a heart-to-heart conversation with the man about his journey to redemption. "Listen," she said, "I love you, but I can't keep walking this road to redemption alone. We need to find a way to support each other, to remain committed to the journey no matter how difficult it may be."

The man listened, realizing that he had burdened Emily with the weight of his journey. He apologized, and together, they worked on finding a way to move forward.

They decided to traverse the long road to redemption together. Emily knew she loved the man and was committed to supporting him as he embarked on the journey of healing and growth.

In the end, Emily learned that the road to redemption can indeed be long and challenging. However, she also discovered the importance of staying committed to the journey, supporting each other, and believing in the power of second chances. Armed with these lessons, she felt ready to face whatever challenges life had to offer.

23 ▌

Chapter 23: The Hope for Forgiveness

Emily had always been someone who believed in the power of forgiveness, both for herself and others.

One day, Emily met a man who would challenge everything she knew about herself. Charismatic, charming, and harboring a dark secret, he intrigued her.

As they started dating, Emily found herself immersed in the man's passion and mysterious nature. She felt like she had finally encountered someone who not only understood her but could also share her love for excitement and thrill.

However, as their relationship deepened, Emily realized that the man was concealing something from her — mistakes from his past that he struggled to forgive himself for.

Despite her deep love for him, Emily couldn't shake the burden of his guilt. It felt like she was carrying the weight of his past mistakes, and she didn't know how to guide him toward forgiveness.

In the end, Emily had a heart-to-heart conversation with the man about his need for forgiveness. "Listen," she said, "I love you, but

I can see that you're carrying a heavy weight of guilt. You need to forgive yourself, to let go of the past."

While the man listened, he seemed unsure of how to find forgiveness. He continued to grapple with self-blame for his past mistakes, and Emily felt like she was losing him.

Eventually, Emily realized that she couldn't make the man forgive himself. Forgiveness was a personal journey he had to undertake.

She made the difficult decision to walk away, understanding that she couldn't sacrifice her own well-being for his. Recognizing that he needed to find his own path to forgiveness, Emily understood she couldn't be the one to save him.

Emily learned that forgiveness is a journey each person must take individually. She knew that to protect herself, she had to trust her instincts, set healthy boundaries, and always prioritize her own well-being.

Top of Form

Chapter 24: The Road to Healing

Emily had been through a lot in her life, from falling in love to narrowly escaping danger. But through it all, she had always been someone who believed in the power of healing and growth.

One day, Emily met a man who would challenge everything she knew about herself. Troubled, broken, and with a darkness inside him that she couldn't resist, he intrigued her.

As they started dating, Emily found herself immersed in the man's pain and his desire for healing. She felt like she had finally encountered someone who not only understood her but could also share her love for healing and growth.

However, as their relationship deepened, Emily began to realize that the man's healing journey was going to be long and difficult. He was grappling with addiction, past trauma, and a deep sense of shame.

Despite her love for the man, Emily couldn't help but feel overwhelmed by the magnitude of his journey. She sensed that a challenging road lay ahead, and she questioned whether she had the strength to stay by his side.

In the end, Emily had a heart-to-heart conversation with the man about his journey to healing. "Listen," she said, "I love you, but I can't keep walking this road to healing alone. We need to find a way to support each other, to stay committed to the journey, no matter how difficult it may be."

The man listened, realizing that he had burdened Emily with the weight of his journey. He apologized, and they worked together to find a way to move forward.

They would still walk the long road to healing, but now they would do so together. Emily knew that she loved the man and was committed to supporting him as he worked towards healing and growth.

In the end, Emily learned that the road to healing can be long and difficult, but it's crucial to stay committed to the journey, support each other, and believe in the power of growth and transformation. She knew that with the lessons she had learned, she was ready to face anything that life had to offer.

Chapter 25: A New Beginning

Emily had been through a lot in her life, from falling in love to narrowly escaping danger. However, throughout these experiences, she remained someone who believed in the power of new beginnings.

One day, Emily met a man who would challenge everything she knew about herself. Troubled, broken, and harboring a darkness inside him that she couldn't resist, he intrigued her.

As they started dating, Emily found herself immersed in the man's pain and his desire for a new beginning. She felt like she had finally encountered someone who not only understood her but could also share her love for healing and growth.

Yet, as their relationship deepened, Emily began to realize that the man's darkness was more intense than she had ever imagined. He grappled with addiction, past trauma, and a deep sense of hopelessness.

Despite her love for the man, Emily couldn't help but feel consumed by his despair. She sensed that she was drowning in his pain and didn't know how to help him.

In the end, Emily had a heart-to-heart conversation with the man about his darkness. "Listen," she said, "I love you, but I can't keep drowning in your pain. You need to seek help, to find a way to start a new beginning."

The man listened, realizing that change was necessary. He began therapy, joined a support group, and worked on addressing his addiction and trauma.

Supported by Emily every step of the way, they started seeing progress. The man opened up to Emily, sharing his fears and hopes, and they grew closer than ever before.

Ultimately, Emily and the man found a new beginning—one built on honesty, trust, and a commitment to healing and growth. Aware of the challenges ahead, they were ready to face them together.

Emily learned that new beginnings can be daunting, but they also offer opportunities for growth and transformation. With the lessons she had learned, she knew she was ready to face anything that life had to offer.

Chapter 26: Forever in Breathless Desire

Emily had experienced a myriad of life events, from falling in love to narrowly escaping danger. Throughout it all, she remained someone who fervently believed in the power of love.

One day, Emily encountered a man who would challenge every aspect of her being. He was charming, affectionate, and had an unwavering passion for living life to the fullest.

As they commenced their journey together, Emily found herself enveloped in the man's love and magnetic nature. She felt a deep connection, finally discovering someone who resonated with her, sharing her fervor for passion and romance.

As their relationship deepened, Emily came to the profound realization that this man was the one she had been searching for her entire life—the one destined to be her forever. He became the person with whom she wanted to spend the rest of her days.

Together, they shared their hopes and dreams, navigated through fears and struggles, and built a life filled with passion, love, and joy.

For Emily, the man represented her forever, and she embraced the certainty of a future together, characterized by breathless desire.

Grateful for every shared moment, laughter, tear, and instance of passion and romance, Emily knew that she had found enduring love.

Armed with the lessons she had learned, the love she had discovered, and the shared commitment, she felt prepared to face anything life had to offer. Hand in hand, they would step into the future, forever bound by breathless desire.

Milton Keynes UK
Ingram Content Group UK Ltd.
UKHW011040240124
436589UK00003B/31